The Peanut Butter Party

Greg Roza

NEIGHBORHOOD READERS

Rosen Classroom Books & Materials™

New York

"Hi, Grape Jelly," said Peanut Butter.
"Come in!"
"Come to the peanut butter party!"

"Hi, Bread," said Peanut Butter.
"Come in! Come to my party!"
"Let's play some music!" said Bread.

Milk came to the party.
"Hi, Milk," said Peanut Butter.
"Come in!"
"Let's dance!" said Milk.

"Hi, Banana," said Peanut Butter.
"Come in!"
"Yes, let's make sandwiches!" they said.